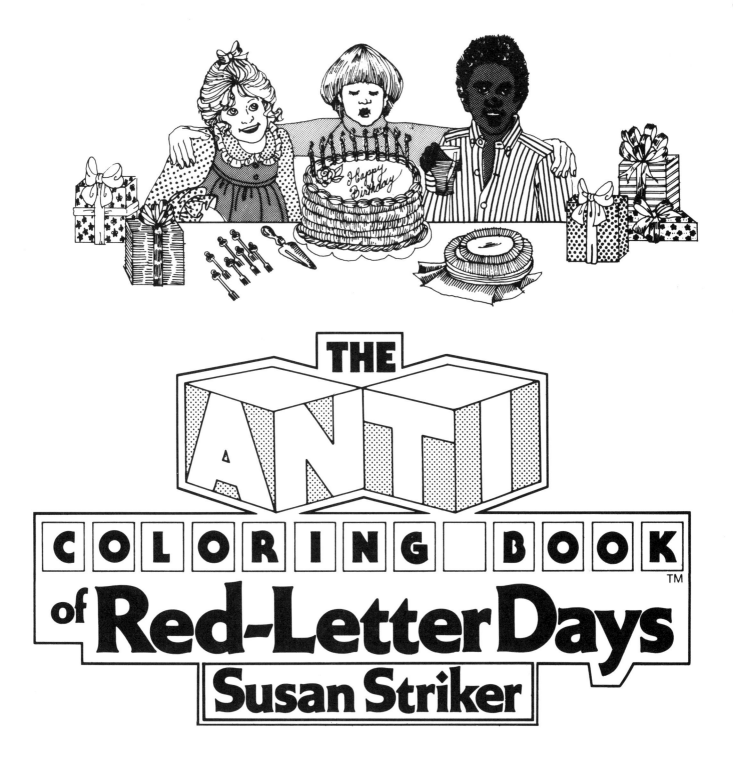

THE ANTI COLORING BOOK ™
of Red-Letter Days
Susan Striker

HOLT, RINEHART and WINSTON   New York

To Carmen Sierra and Pat Feller

this is the law:
no sames
no same leaves
pebble persons
places time faces
grasses
whoever disobeys the law
gets bored.

–Anonymous

Published by Holt, Rinehart and Winston,
383 Madison Avenue, New York, New York 10017.
Published simultaneously in Canada by
Holt, Rinehart and Winston of Canada, Limited.

ISBN: 0-03-057873-6

First Edition

Printed in the United States of America
10 9 8 7 6 5 4 3 2 1

Illustrations by Brent Brolin, Judy Francis, Steve Hall, James Janey,
Randi Katzman, George Love, Maggie MacGowan, Susan Striker, and
David Vozar.

Introduction

One of the most important aspects of an art activity is the extent to which a child can personally identify with it. Any event that has meaning for a child is a natural subject for an art experience. Because of their built-in excitement, holidays are ideal opportunities for encouraging creativity and expressing feelings. At the same time, through art, children can get closer to the significance of a holiday. Thanksgiving can be an occasion for thoughtful contemplation. What better way is there to explore fantasies, express fears, or vent hostilities than in a Halloween mask? And who does not feel special when a birthday comes around?

Sadly, year after year children work on a dreary procession of adult-directed clichés via standardized copy work and patterns. Too many children today see only plastic pumpkins and buy only ready-made Valentine cards. Each time I pass a school-room window plastered with identical Thanksgiving turkeys or cut-out triangular Christmas trees neatly lined up, I wonder at the many missed opportunities for personal involvement and creative expression, and the wasted chances to teach children about society's traditions. The family that favors store-bought holiday decorations over the lopsided ones their young children make is missing out on a good chance for communication and fun.

The projects in *The Anti-Coloring Book of Red-Letter Days* are meant to stimulate thinking and feeling, and, I hope, will generate other kinds of more personalized holiday celebrations. "Design your own Halloween mask" might inspire children to do just that after finishing their drawings; "Decorate this Christmas tree with unusual ornaments you have made" could lead to some fun-filled evenings. Ideally, parents and teachers will reject prepackaged busy work misnamed "art" in favor of children's spontaneous designs. I would like to see both children and adults proudly display work that represents something more of themselves.

New Year's Resolution

恭喜發財

HAPPY
NEW
YEAR

恭喜發財

© Susan Striker

These children are enjoying the
Chinese New Year celebration.

If the groundhog comes out and sees its shadow on Groundhog Day, spring will come in six weeks. What is your favorite thing about spring?

© Susan Striker

Design a valentine for your best friend.

George Washington's honesty was praised
when he admitted chopping down his father's cherry tree.
What was the worst mischief you ever had to admit?

© Susan Striker

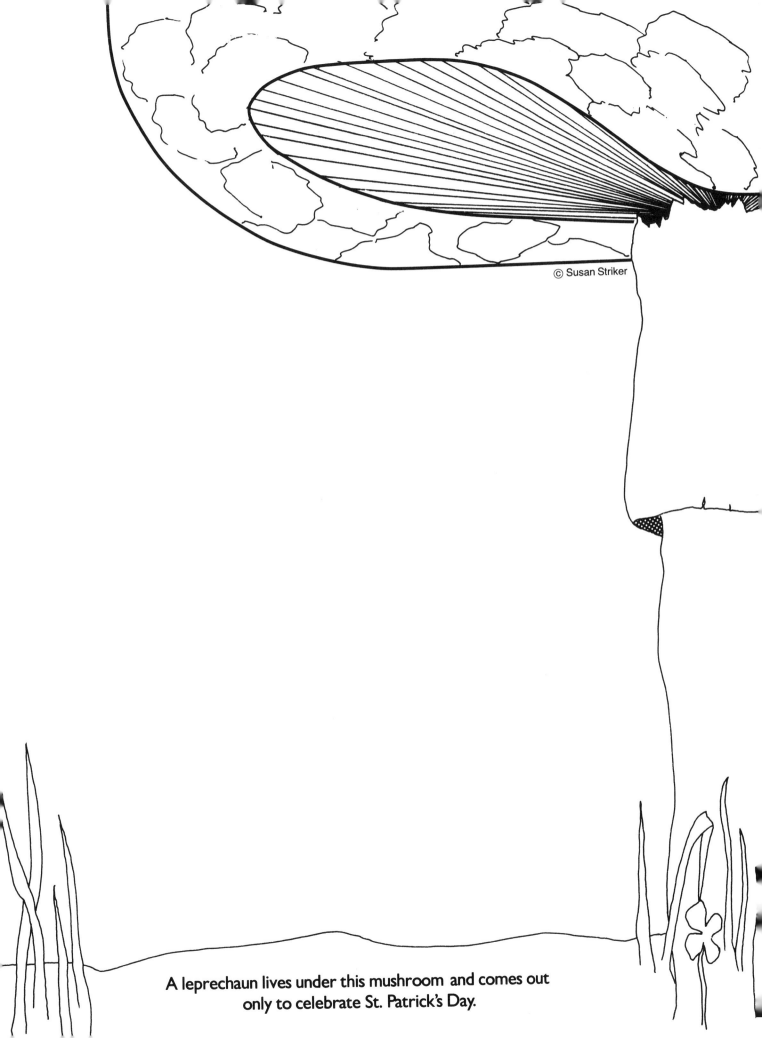

© Susan Striker

A leprechaun lives under this mushroom and comes out
only to celebrate St. Patrick's Day.

Today is April 1

Homework

Read chapter 2

What joke can you play on April Fool's Day?

Decorate this basketful of Easter eggs.

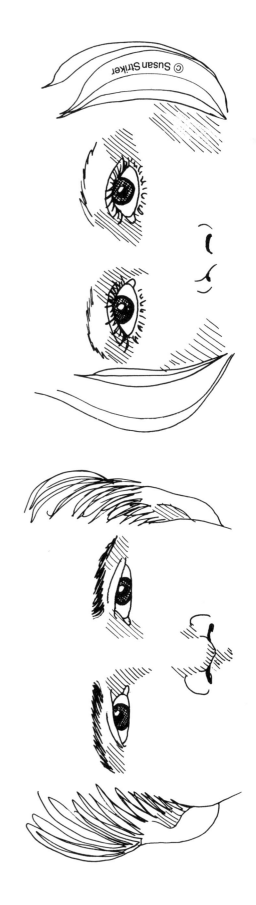

Turn the page and show what Easter bonnets
these folks are modeling for us.

© Susan Striker

**What will you wish for when you blow out
the candles on your birthday cake?**

**At your next birthday party, a magician will surprise
your friends by pulling something very unusual out of a hat.**

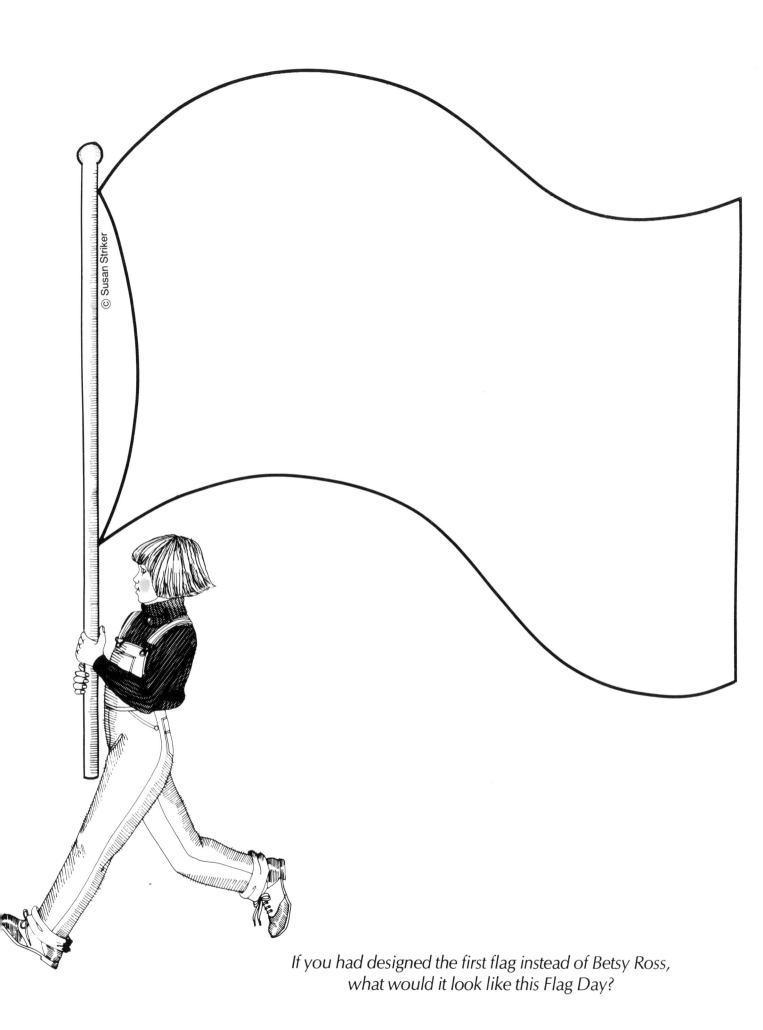

© Susan Striker

*If you had designed the first flag instead of Betsy Ross,
what would it look like this Flag Day?*

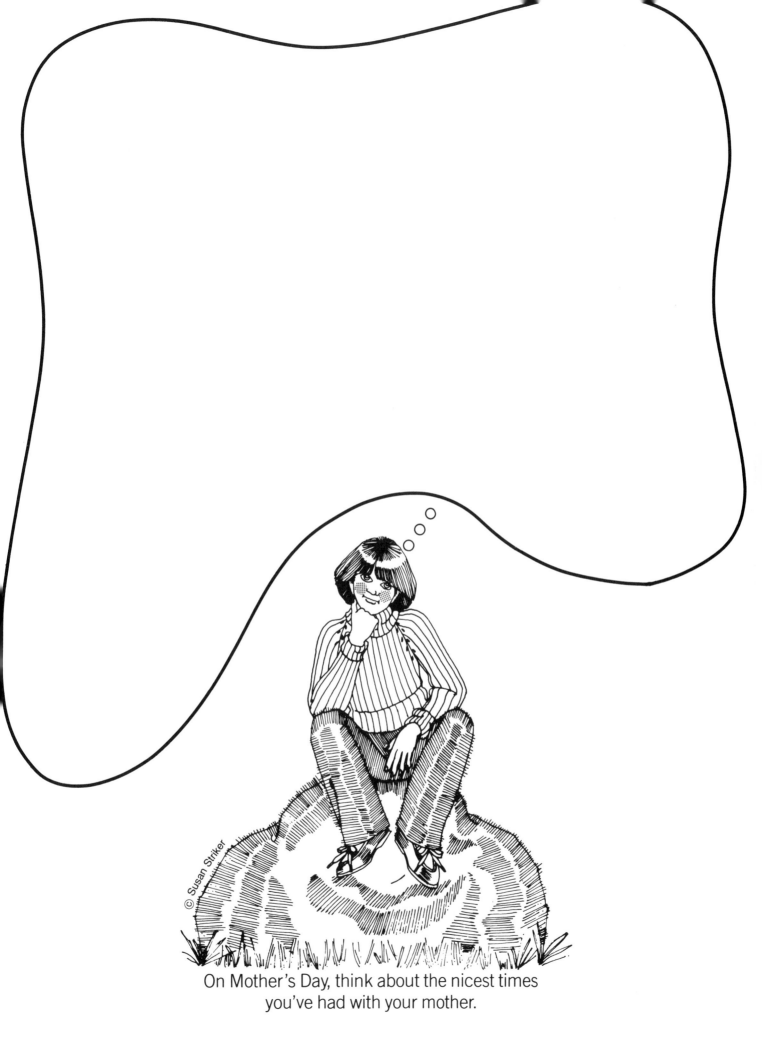

On Mother's Day, think about the nicest times
you've had with your mother.

© Susan Striker

Design
a float for the
Puerto Rican Day
parade.

© Susan Striker

© Susan Striker

What special thing will you do
for your dad on Father's Day?

Produce the fireworks to celebrate
the Fourth of July.

© Susan Striker

**On Independence Day,
think of what's the best thing
about living in the United States.**

On Halloween a horrible monster
will appear at your door.

Carve a jack-o-lantern's face on this pumpkin.

What is this witch brewing?

Design your own Halloween mask.

© Susan Striker

**You won first prize in
the Halloween costume contest.**

© Susan Striker

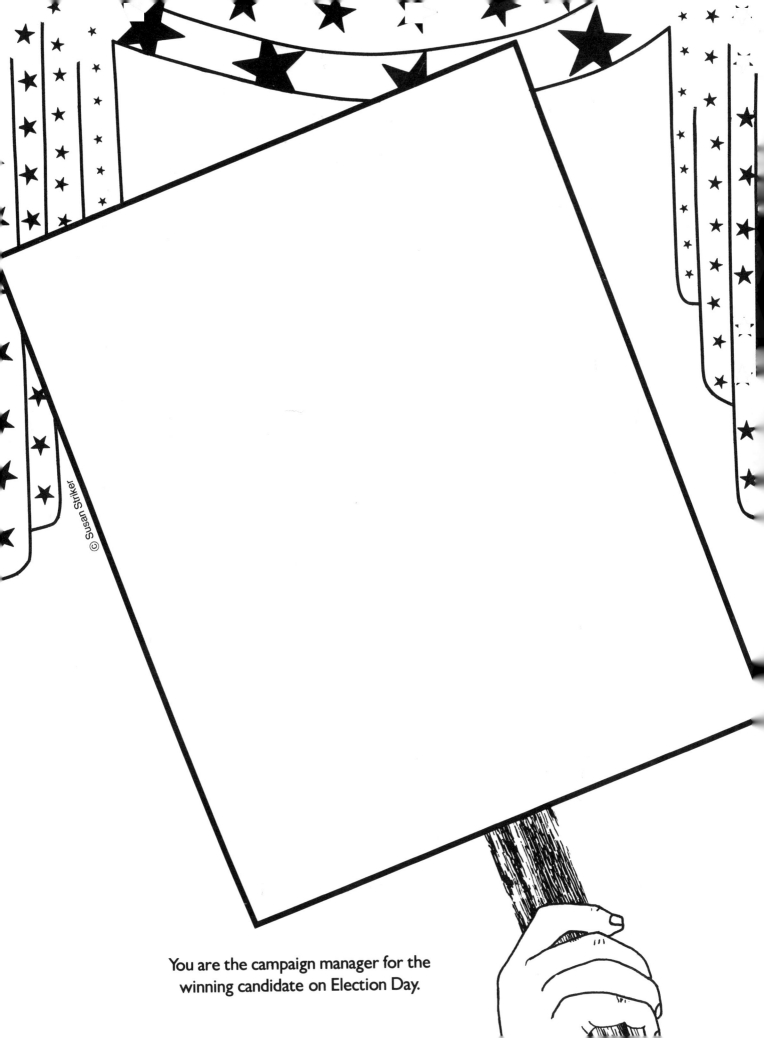

You are the campaign manager for the
winning candidate on Election Day.

What are you thankful for this Thanksgiving?

On Hannukah we celebrate one of life's miracles.
Which of life's miracles do you think is most wonderful?

© Susan Striker

What will you do with your
Hannukah gelt (money)?

You have been hired to decorate the Christmas windows
in the town's biggest department store.

© Susan Striker

Decorate this Christmas tree with unusual ornaments you have made.

What stocking stuffers are fun to receive?

What would you like Santa to bring this year?